O o

Oscar, Me, and the Letter O

Alphabet Friends

by Cynthia Klingel and Robert B. Noyed

The Child's World®

The Child's World®

**Published in the United States of America
by The Child's World**®
P.O. Box 326
Chanhassen, MN 55317-0326
800-599-READ
www.childsworld.com

The Child's World®: Mary Berendes, Publishing Director

Editorial Directions, Inc.: E. Russell Primm, Editorial
Director; Emily Dolbear, Line Editor; Ruth Martin,
Editorial Assistant; Linda S. Koutris, Photo Researcher
and Selector

Photographs ©: Corbis/Picture Quest: Cover & 11;
Digital Vision/Picture Quest: 12; Jacqui Hurst/Corbis:
15; Ron Sanford/Corbis: 16; Carin Krasner/Corbis: 19;
C Squared Studios/Photodisc/Getty Images: 20.

Library of Congress Cataloging-in-Publication Data
Klingel, Cynthia Fitterer.
  Oscar, me, and the letter O / by Cynthia Klingel and
Robert B. Noyed.
     p. cm. — (Alphabet readers)
Summary: A simple story about a lonely boy named
Oscar introduces the letter "o".
  ISBN 1-59296-105-3 (Library Bound : alk. paper)
  [1. Loneliness—Fiction. 2. Alphabet.] I. Noyed, Robert
B., ill. II. Title.
  PZ7.K6798Os 2003
  [E]—dc21
                                    2003006604

Note to parents and educators:
The first skill children acquire before becoming successful readers is individual letter recognition. The Alphabet Friends series has been created with the needs of young learners in mind. Each engaging book begins by showing the difference between the capital letter and the lowercase letter. In each of the books on the vowels and the consonants c and g, children are introduced to the different sounds that the letter can make. Finally, children see that the letters can be found at the beginning of a word, in the middle of a word, and in most cases, at the end of a word.

Following the introduction, children meet their Alphabet Friends. The friend in each story encounters many words that include the featured letter of that book. Each noun that begins with the title letter is highlighted in red with the initial letter of the word in bold. Above the word is a rebus drawing that establishes a strong picture cue.

At the end of each book, we have included three words lists. Can your young learners find all the words in each book with the title letter in them?

Let's learn about the letter O.

The letter O can look like this: O.

4

The letter **O** can also look like this: **o.**

The letter o makes two different sounds.

One sound is the long sound,

like in the word ocean.

ocean

The other sound is the short sound,

like in the word otter.

otter

The letter **o** can be at the beginning of a word, like one.

one

The letter **o** can be in the middle of a word, like horn.

h**o**rn

The letter o can be at the

end of a word, like igloo.

igloo

One day **O**scar was lonely. His older

brother was busy playing his **o**boe.

What could **O**scar do?

At **o**ne o'clock, **O**scar phoned me. I

came over. **O**scar and I went outside.

We took a walk to the **o**cean.

At the **o**cean, **O**scar and I looked for

oysters. By three o'clock, we had found

only one **o**yster. **O**scar and I went back

to the house.

Oscar and I read some books. One

book was about an oily otter. Another

book was about ostriches. Did you

know ostriches are the largest living

birds in the world?

The phone rang. It was my mother. It

was time for me to go home. See you

later, Oscar!

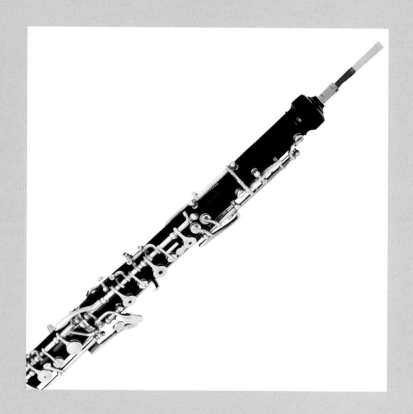

Finally it was four o'clock. **O**scar's

brother opened his door. He was

done playing his **o**boe. Now **O**scar

was not alone!

Fun Facts

An adult **o**strich can weigh as much as 345 pounds (156 kilograms)—that's heavier than a baby elephant! **O**striches cannot fly, but they can run at very high speeds. **O**striches have to run fast to escape their enemies, which include lions and cheetahs.

The **o**tter is an aquatic mammal—that means it spends a lot of time in the water. **O**tters are excellent swimmers. They live along rivers, streams, lakes, in marshes, and in the ocean near the shore. **O**tters spend a lot of time playing, and express their feelings with a variety of different sounds.

Oysters are known for two things—their valuable pearls and their great taste. The beautiful pearls used in jewelry and in other decorative ways are made mostly by just one kind of **o**yster—the pearl **o**yster. Other **o**ysters may form pearls, but they are not the right shape and color to make them valuable. **O**ysters are also considered a delicious food.

To Read More

About the Letter O
Flanagan, Alice K. *Hot Spot: The Sound of O.* Chanhassen, Minn.: The Child's World, 2000.
Noyed, Robert B., and Cynthia Klingel. *On My Boat: The Sound of Long O.* Chanhassen, Minn.: The Child's World, 2000.

About Ostriches
Simon, Francesca, and Neal Layton (illustrator). *Three Cheers for Ostrich!* London: Gullane Children's Books, 2001.
Whitehouse, Patricia. *Ostrich.* Chicago: Heinemann Library, 2003.

About Otters
Berger, Barbara Helen. *A Lot of Otters.* New York: Philomel Books, 1997.
Pledger, Maurice. *An Adventure with Oscar Otter.* San Diego, Calif.: Silver Dolphin Books, 1998.

About Oysters
Reese, Bob. *Oola Oyster: Story and Pictures.* Chicago: Childrens Press, 1983.
Tate, Suzanne, and James Melvin (illustrator). *Perlie Oyster: A Tale of an Amazing Oyster.* Nags Head, N.C.: Nags Head Art, 1989.

Words with O

Words with O at the Beginning
oboe
ocean
o'clock
of
oily
older
one
only
opened
Oscar
ostriches
otter
outside
over
oyster
oysters

Words with O in the Middle
about
alone
another
book
books
brother
could
door
done
for
found
four
home
horn
house
igloo
know
lonely
long
look
looked
mother
mow
oboe
o'clock
phone
phoned
short
some
sound
sounds
took
word
world
you

Words with O at the End
also
do
go
igloo
to
two

About the Authors

Cynthia Klingel has worked as a high school English teacher and an elementary teacher. She is currently the curriculum director for a Minnesota school district. Cynthia Klingel lives with her family in Mankato, Minnesota.

Robert B. Noyed started his career as a newspaper reporter. Since then, he has worked in communications and public relations for a Minnesota school district for more than fourteen years. Robert B. Noyed lives with his family in Brooklyn Center, Minnesota.